WESTMINSTER SCHOOLS

SMYTHE GAMBRELL
LIBRARY

PRESENTED BY

Dale Maffett
In honor of
fletcher maffett
1988

T.T.

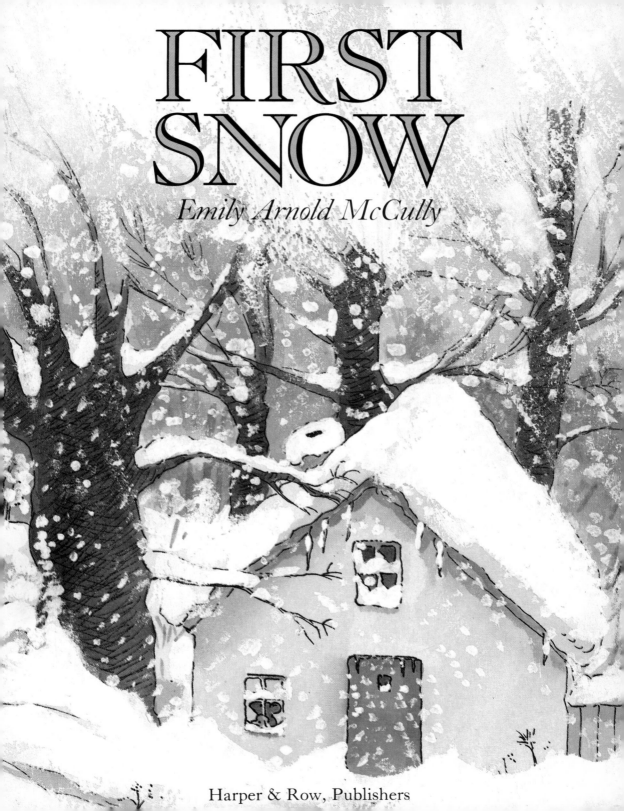

FIRST SNOW

Emily Arnold McCully

Harper & Row, Publishers

Library of Congress Cataloging in Publication Data
McCully, Emily Arnold.
  First snow.
  Summary: A timid little mouse discovers the
thrill of sledding in the first snow of the winter.
  1. Children's stories, American. [1. Mice—
Fiction. 2. Snow—Fiction. 3. Stories without
words] I. Title.
PZ7.M478415Fi 1985   [E]   84-43244
ISBN 0-06-024128-4   ISBN 0-06-024129-2 (lib. bdg.)

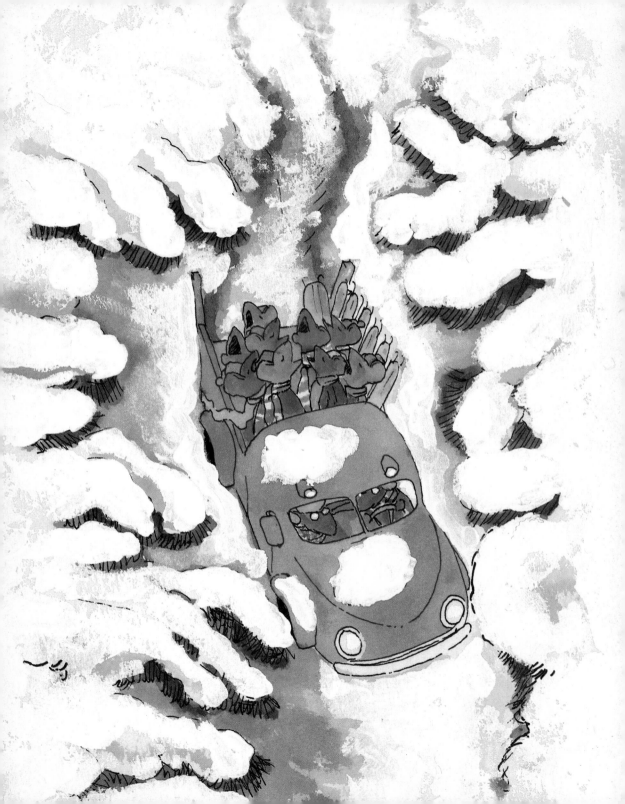

10.65